MATCH EACH ITEM WITH ITS CORRESPONDI~~NG~~

FOLLOW THE DOTTED LINE TO MAKE THE SHAPES

HELP THE CHARACTERS TO GET HOME

MATCH EACH ITEM WITH ITS CORRESPONDING COLOR

DRAW A LINE TO MATCH AND COMPLETE THE HALLOWEEN ITEMS

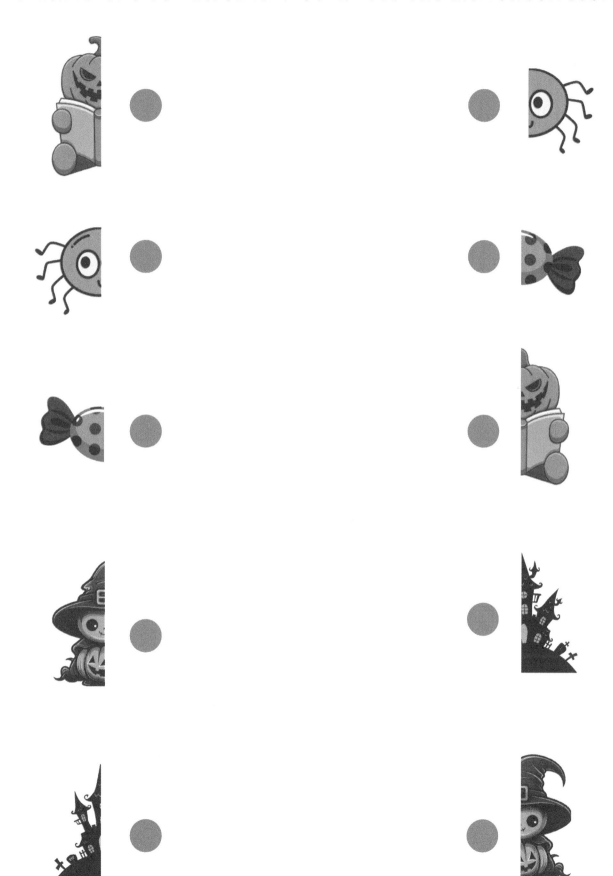

FIND THE MYSTERIOUS SHADOW

COLOR EACH WHITE CIRCLE WITH THE CORRESPONDING COLOR DEFINED

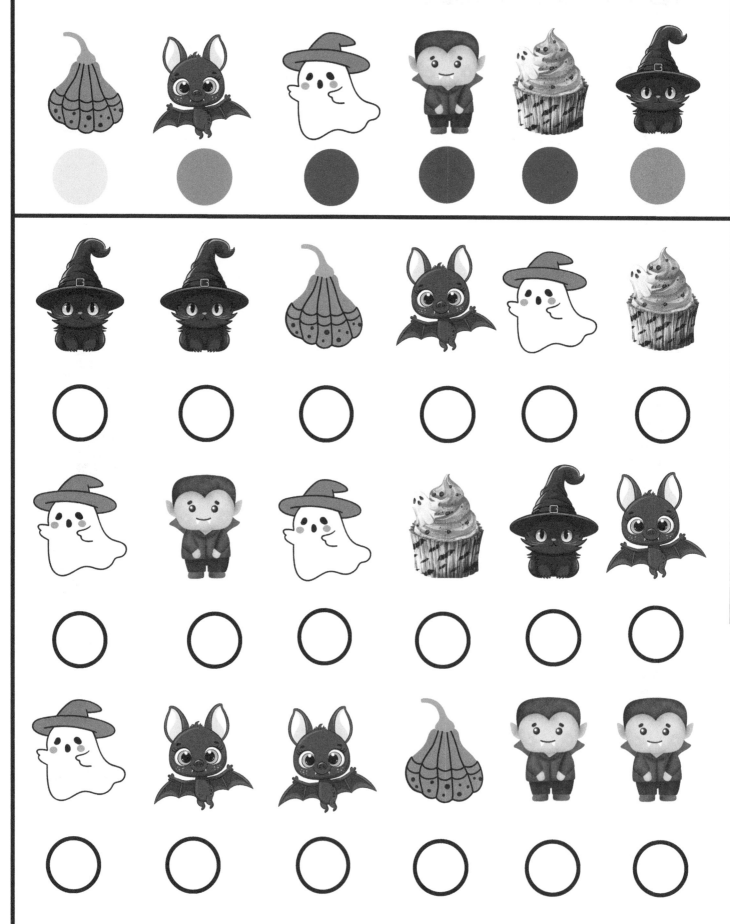

PUT THE CORRESPONDENT SIGN BELOW UNDER EACH CANDY

●	+	I	−

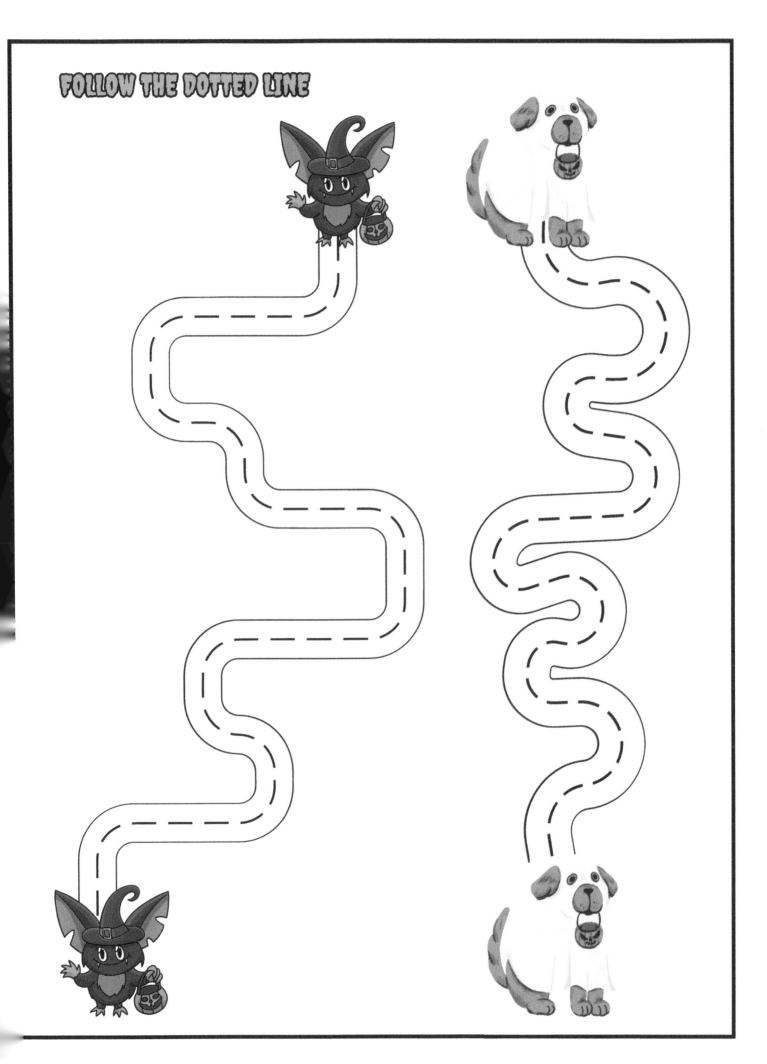

FOLLOW THE DOTTED LINE

COLOR EACH ITEM AS SHOWN IN THE FIRST ROW

FOLOW THE LINE TO DISCOVER THE HALLOWEEN WORLD

CIRCLE THE BIGGER VERSION

FILL APPROPRIATE COLORS IN THE BLANK CIRCLES TO COMPLETE THE PATTERNS

TRACE THE DOTTED LINE

SEARCH THE HALLOWEEN ITEMS

WHERE IS THIS GOST? →

MATCH EACH ITEM WITH ITS CORRESPONDING

FOLLOW THE DOTTED LINE TO DISCOVER THE HALLOWEEN WORLD

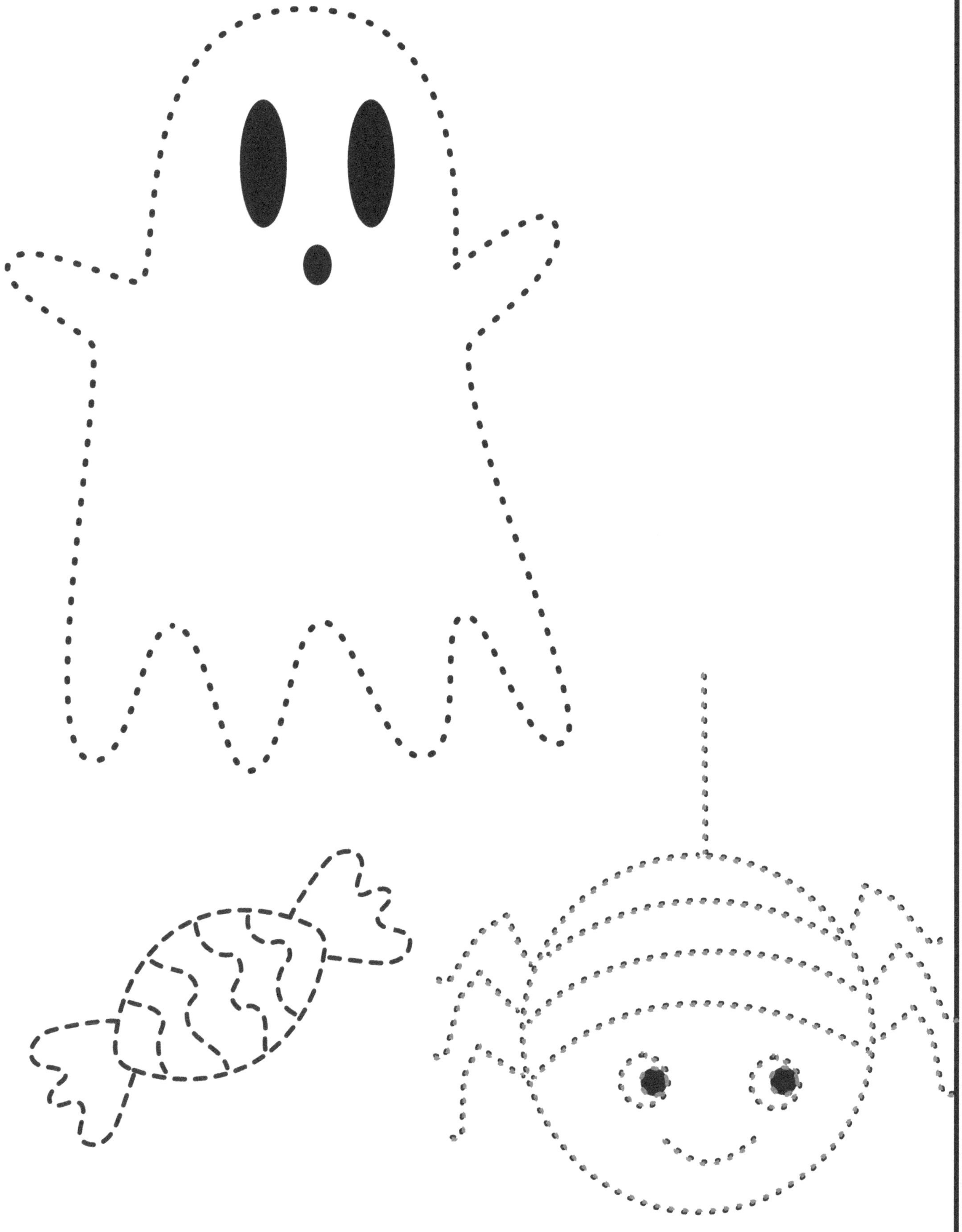

COLOR YOUR OWN SPECIAL HAT FOR HALLOWEEN

CIRCLE THE SMALLEST VERSION

CHOOSE THE CORRESPONDING SHADOW OF EACH HAT

WHAT'S NEXT?

FOLLOW THE DOTTED LINE WITH THE INDICATED COLOR

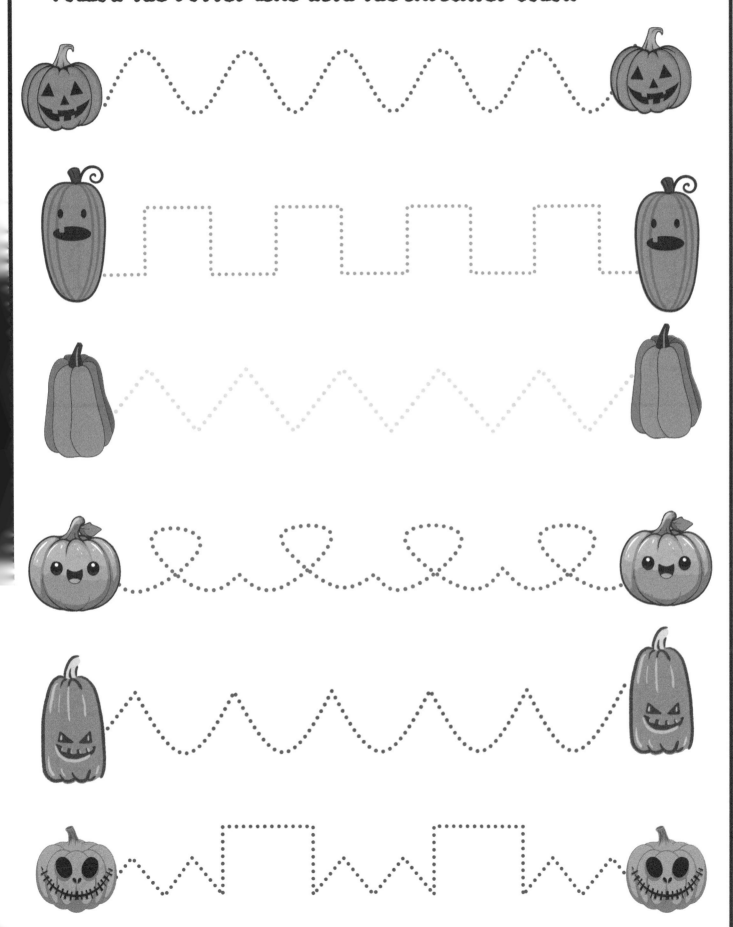

IDENTIFY AND COLOR THE DIFFERENT ITEM FROM EACH ROW

DRAW THE PUMPKIN WITH THE DEFINED COLORS

DRAW THE SHAPES WITH THE INDICATED COLORS

DRAW A LINE BETWEEN THE SQUARES AND ITS CORRESPONDING NUMBERS

DRAW LINES TO GET THE SAME CANDY PATTERN AS THE FIRST ONE

FOLLOW THE DOTS TO WRITE THE NUMBER

FOLLOW THE DOTS TO WRITE THE NUMBER

4 4 4 4 4

FOLLOW THE DOTS TO WRITE THE NUMBER

FOLLOW THE DOTTED LINE

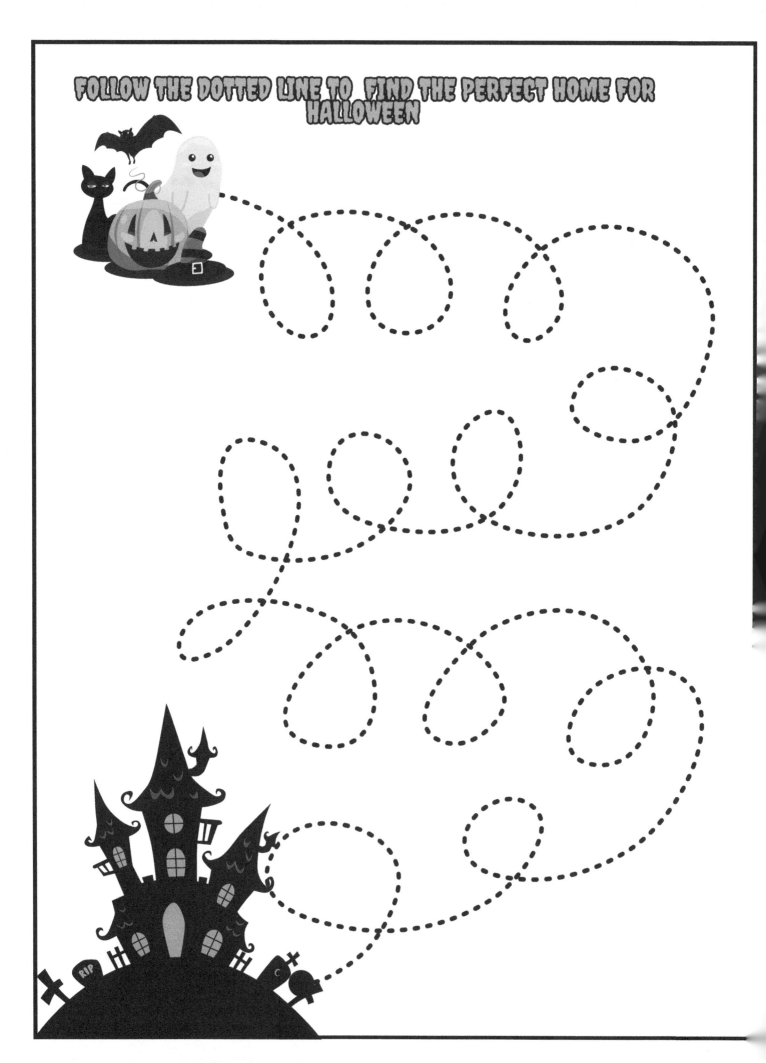

FOLLOW THE DOTTED LINE TO FIND THE PERFECT HOME FOR HALLOWEEN

WHICH ONE IS DIFFERENT?

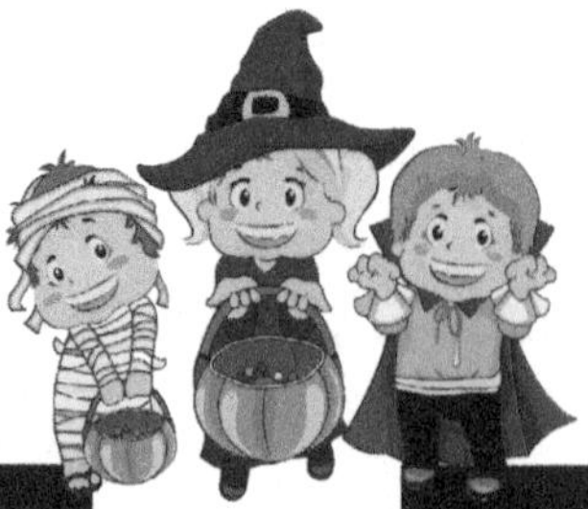

FIND THE WAY TO THE CANDIES

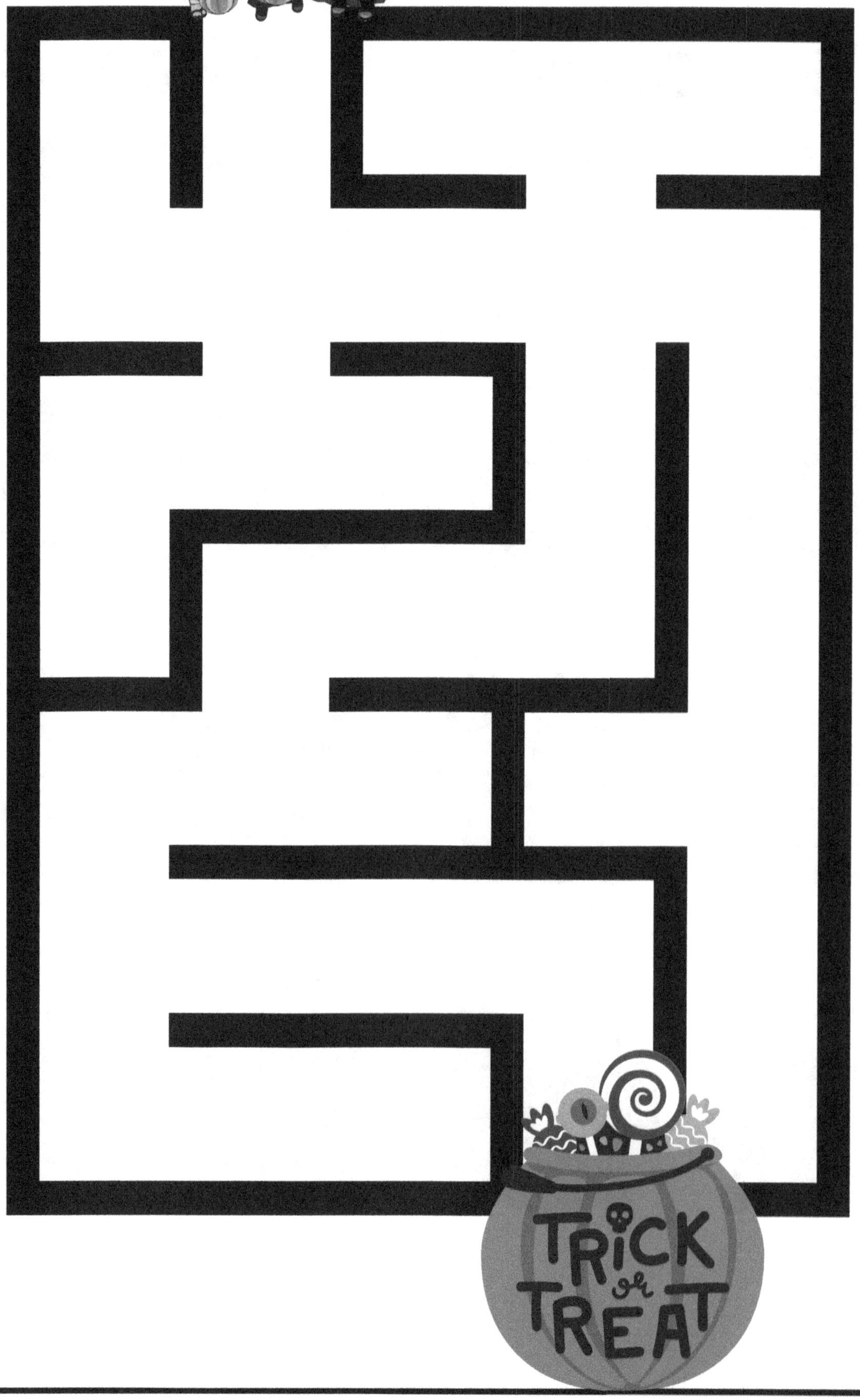

COLOR THE SMALLEST OBJECT IN EACH GROUP

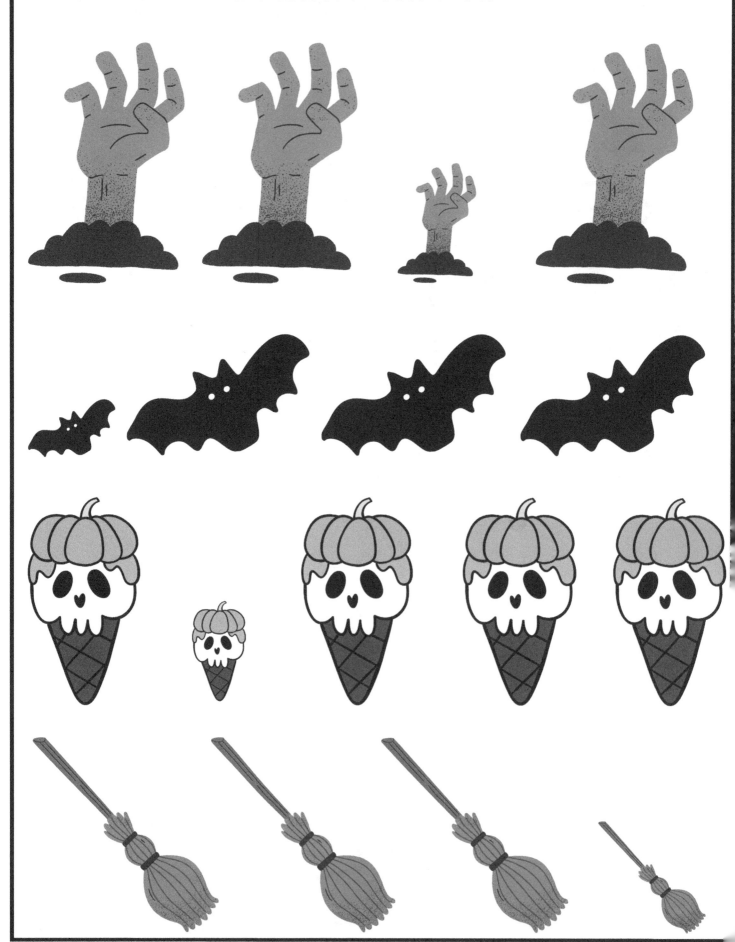

CIRCLE THE CORRECT GROUP OF ITEMS

1

2

3

MATCH EACH ITEM WITH ITS CORRESPONDING

COLOR THE BIGGER OBJECT FROM EACH ROW

HOW MANY TO THE LEFT AND HOW MANY TO THE RIGHT?

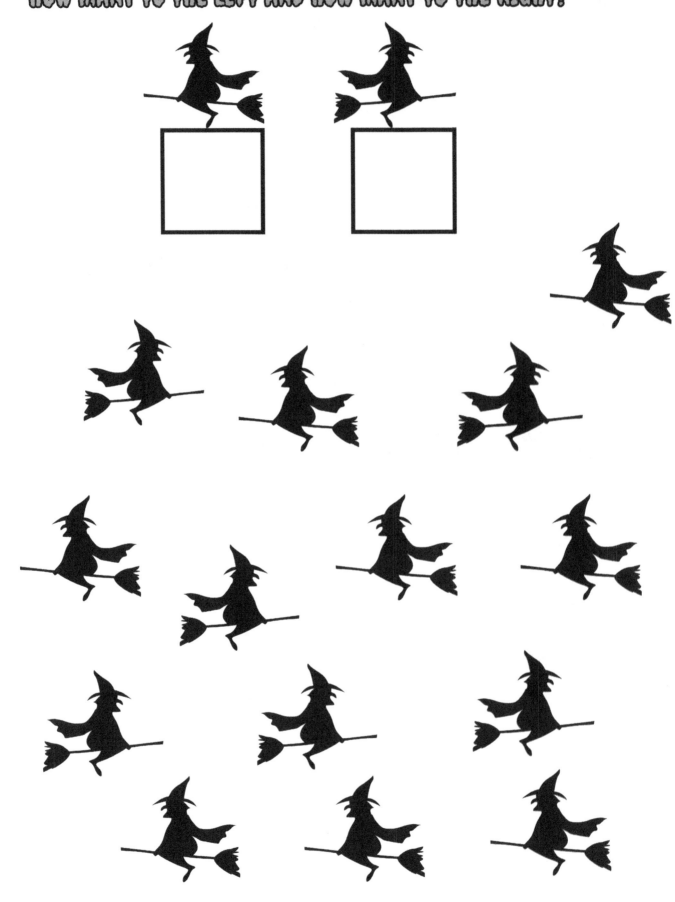

HOW MANY GO UP AND HOW MANY GO DOWN?

MATCH EACH PICTURE WITH ITS CORESPONDING DIRECTION

FOLLOW THE NUMBERS TO DISCOVER HALOWEEN ITEM

FOLLOW THE NUMBERS TO DISCOVER HALOWEEN ITEM

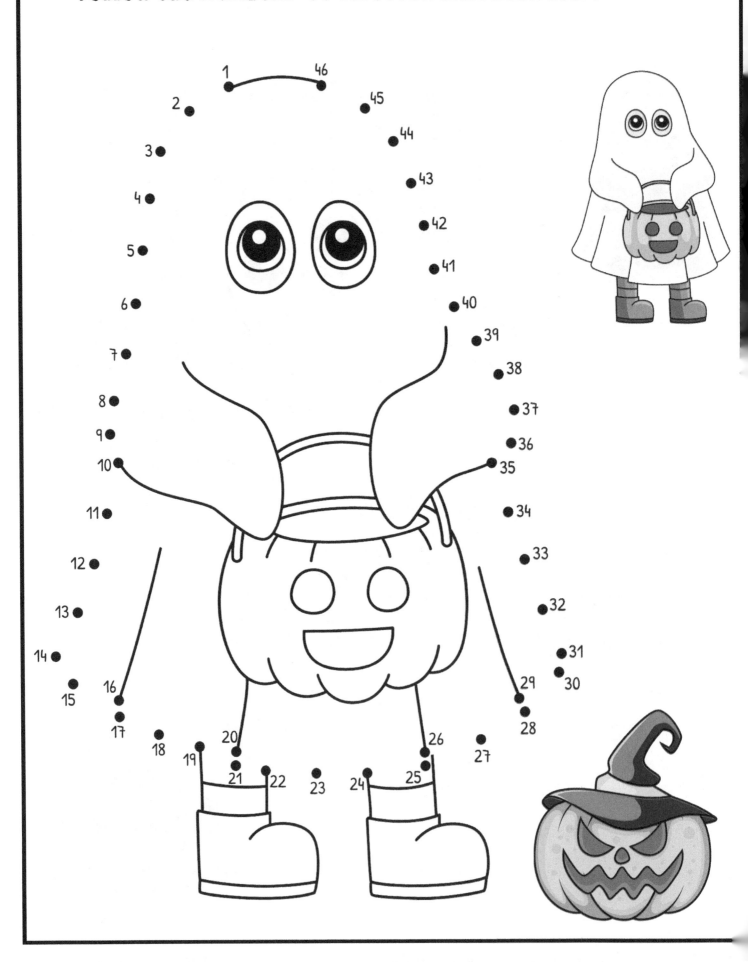

FOLLOW THE NUMBERS TO DISCOVER HALOWEEN ITEM

HELP THE BOY TO GET THE SWEETS

COLOR THE HALOWEEN GIRL

WHICH PUMPKIN IS SCARED?

FOLLOW THE DOTTED LINE TO MAKE THE SHAPES

HAVE FUN WITH COLORS

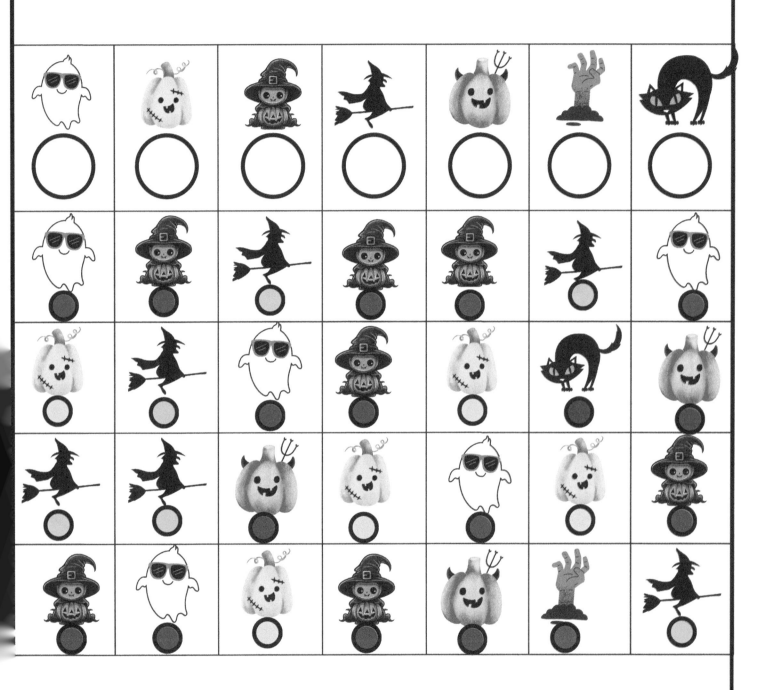

HAVE FUN WITH COLORS

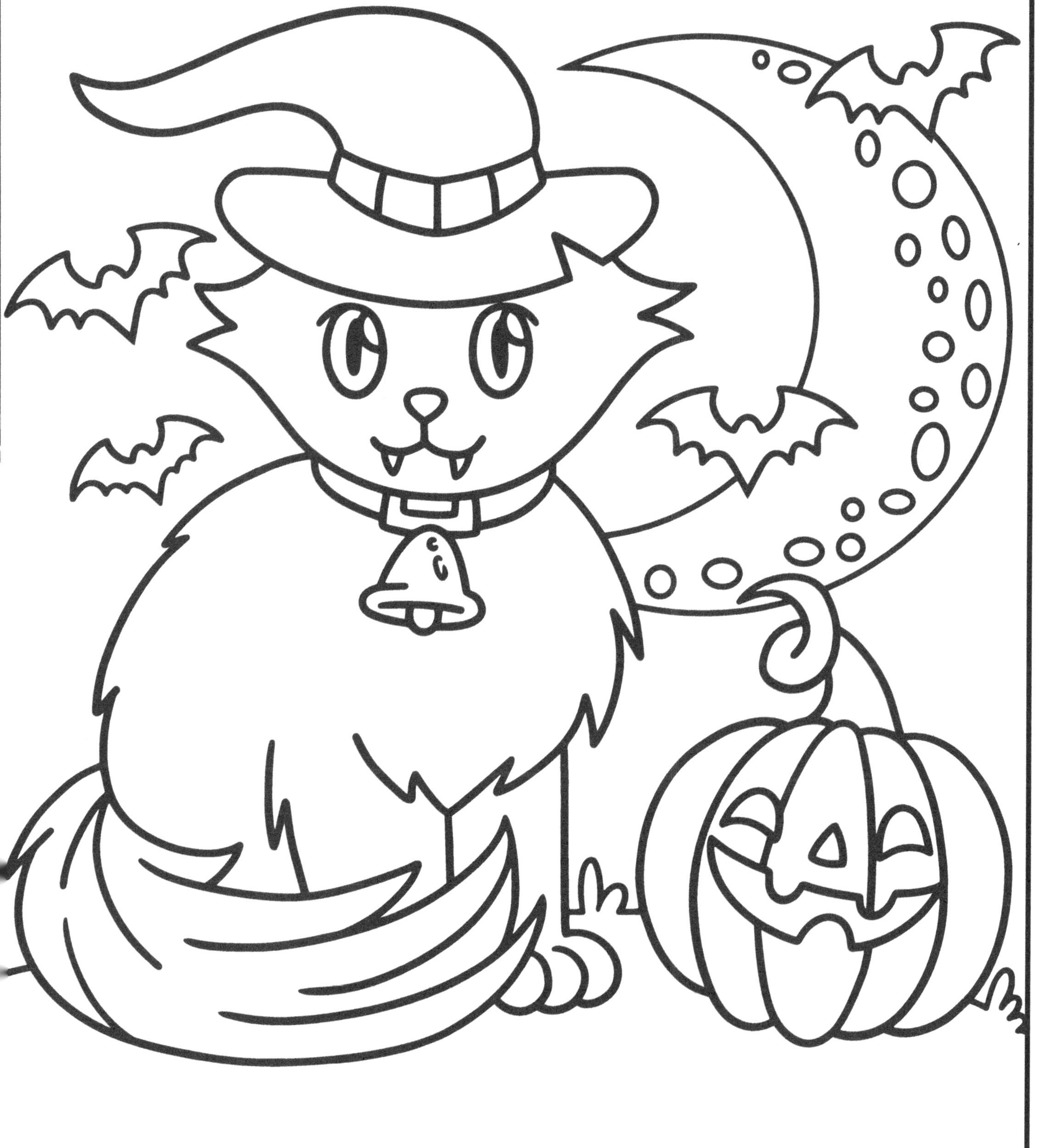

HELP THE GOST TO GET TO SWEETS

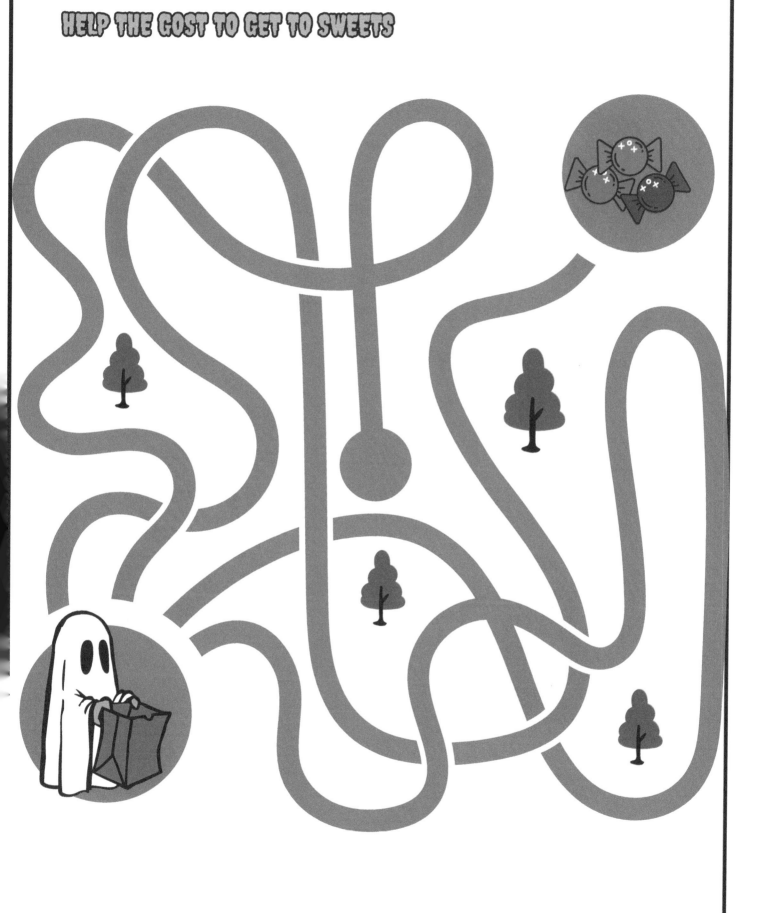

DRAW A LINE FROM BIGGER VERSION TO SMALLEST VERSION

Made in the USA
Las Vegas, NV
19 October 2023